THE MYSTERY OF HAUNTED TREE

THE MYSTERY OF HAUNTED TREE

APOORVA SHARMA

PAPER TOWNS
PUBLISHERS

PAPER TOWNS
PUBLISHERS

First published by

Papertowns Publishers
72, Vishwanath Dham Colony,
Niwaru Road, Jhotwara,
Jaipur, 302012

The Mystery of Haunted Tree

ISBN Print Book – 978-93-6185-774-4

Printed in India

CONTENTS

ACKNOWLEDGEMENT

This book is more than just words on paper—it is a dream that took shape with the love and support.

I would like to thank my family and friends, whose unconditional love, encouragement, and faith in me became the foundation of this journey. Without their constant support, this book would never have seen the light of day.

And to my readers—you are the heart of this book. Your time, connection, and belief in my work give meaning to every page written. This book belongs as much to you as it does to me.

With gratitude and love,
Apoorva Sharma

SYNOPSIS

In the small, peaceful village of Sambhar, life is plain, peaceful, and routine-except for one ominous landmark: the "Bhootwala Ped," rumoured to be haunted. For generations, villagers have lived in fear of the tree, going out of their way to travel around it, even if that meant an additional two hours of walking daily.

But when five adventurous children—Rohan, Riya, Aarav, Bunty, and Chintu—make up their minds that they›re fed-up living in fear, curiosity sets off an exciting journey. What starts off as an attempt to debunk the ghost tales soon turns into something much greater.

What is buried beneath the roots might change the history of the village—if the kids have the courage to expose it. Because sometimes the most frightening myths conceal the most amazing truths… and unearthing one enigma might just wake up another.

Mixing humour, suspense, and heart, The Mystery of the Haunted Tree is an enthralling story of friendship, courage, and the magic of transforming childhood curiosity into life-altering discoveries.

CHAPTER 1

THE SHORTCUT NO ONE TAKES

There was a village named Sambhar in Rajasthan—a small, peaceful place where everyone knew everyone; even the cows and buffaloes had unique nicknames. Life here moved slowly, like the hands of the dusty wall clock in panchayat office. There were green fields on all sides, a big banyan tree in the middle, and a chaiwala at the main bus stand who could remember how sweet every person liked their tea. Life over there was simple, grounded and filled with harmless chatter.

Except for one thing.

At the very edge of the village, beside a dense grove of trees, stood something no one talked about too loudly – an old, towering tree that seemed like it didn't belong. Its arms twisted like branches, and its bark was blacker than a rain cloud, and it stood alone—like it hated the rest of the forest. It didn't blend in with the forest. In fact, it stood apart – as it even the other trees were scared of it.

People called it "Bhootwala Ped."

No one remembered how the story started. Some claimed that decades ago, a man had seen a ghost sitting on its branch, humming an old and scary lullaby. Some claimed that they heard some weird laughter at night. Others said glowing eyes stared at anyone who got close.

Even birds avoided its branches. Not a single crow ever dared to sit there. During storms, the other trees bent and danced with the wind, but this one stood rigid – as if it had rooted itself to something more than just soil.

The tree's strange presence might've been forgotten like most old tales, but unfortunately, it stood right on the shortest path to the village school. A narrow trail that cut through the fields, entered the woods for barely a minute, and then emerged near the school gate.

If one took this path, they could reach school in just fifteen minutes. Quick and easy.

But no one took it.

Because no one wanted to go near that tree.

Instead, all the villagers and their children chose the longer road – a sun-baked, uneven stretch that circled around the fields, passed grazing cattle, and went through three sharp turns before finally reaching the school. This route added an extra hour and a half of walking every single day.

Still, no one complained much. Not because they liked it. But because fear had become part of the routine.

Children learned early on to avoid that corner of the village. Mothers warned their kids never to look at the tree directly, especially not at night. If a cricket ball rolled toward the forest, it was considered lost forever.

Strangely, no one had ever seen anything exactly. The stories lived in whispers. Like a shadow you don't talk about, but also don't try to outrun.

The tree, meanwhile, stood there in silence, as if enjoying the fear it commanded.

Years passed. Generations grew up hearing the same bedtime warnings. And slowly, the fear turned into habit. The shortcut became an untold taboo. A mystery wrapped in silence.

But mysteries, no matter how old, always have a way of calling to someone.

And one day, someone would answer.

CHAPTER 2

THE FANTASTIC FIVE

Sambhar was a peaceful village—too quiet, some would say—where even the buffaloes chewed thoughtfully and the crows looked like they were in deep, thoughtful debates. But amid all this peace lived five children who were anything but boring. The villagers called them the Fantastic Five. No one knew who bestowed upon them this nickname, but it stuck like glue.

There was Aarav, the scientist in progress. He once made a rocket using a plastic bottle, vinegar, and baking soda that flew straight into the Pradhan uncle's washing line.

Then there was Riya, the clever girl with sharp eyes and even sharper words—she once convinced a whole group of older boys that she had a magical talking pen that could fulfil all the wishes, only to reveal later it was a regular pen and they were just gullible.

Rohan, the self-appointed leader, was loud, confident, and always ready with a plan for every situation. His energy was contagious, his ideas were wild, and he believed every problem had a solution—even if that solution involved climbing a water tank or jumping into a big river.

Bunty, the slightly scared but entirely lovable one, had a heart bigger than his fear. He cried easily, laughed loudly, and overthought everything, literally everything. But if someone was hurt or in need of help, he'd be the first one to run to their side.

And finally, Chintu, the smallest and the smartest among them all, had a mind that ran faster than his tiny legs. His size made people underestimate him, but his brain could beat anyone in a game of tricks. He once sold an 'invisible pen' to three children for actual money, and they didn't even complain.

The five of them were walking the long, tiring route to school once again, bags bouncing, shoes dragging, and faces expressing all seven stages of mourning grief.

"I swear I'll start writing letters to the ghost," Rohan grumbled. "Dear Ghost, please let us pass. You're painful, Rohan."

You'll probably misspell the ghost and end up calling him a goat," Riya said, half-smiling.

"At least goats don't haunt shortcuts," Bunty whispered nervously, eyeing the forest.

Aarav adjusted his glasses and pointed ahead. "We walk 90 minutes extra every day because no one wants to pass by a tree. A *tree*, not a monster, not a villain from a Bollywood movie—just a really old, tall, and really suspicious tree, which can't move and even can't stretch its arms to catch anyone."

"The Bhootwala ped," Chintu said in a spooky voice, raising his fingers like claws.

Riya looked uneasy. "But Aarav… What if the rumours are true? What if there really is something?"

"Oh, come on, Riya," Aarav replied, amused. "You're the same girl who climbed Babloo Uncle's mango tree in the middle of the night just to prove a point."

"That was different. Babloo Uncle said girls can't climb trees, so I climbed it twice," Riya said proudly.

"Exactly! So don't tell me you're scared of a tree that hasn't even spoken to anyone," Aarav smirked.

Rohan laughed. "Riya, remember when you shouted at that stray dog that stole your chapati? Even the dog gave it back."

"That was a good chapati," she said seriously. "It was full of ghee."

"See? You're the bravest of us all!" Aarav declared.

"Hey! What about me?" Bunty looked offended.

"You cried when the wind blew your hat away," Chintu replied.

"It was my lucky hat," Bunty muttered.

"I'm still braver than Chintu," Bunty said with a smug look.

"Excuse me?" Chintu shot back. "I'm the only one who walked into that haunted house last Diwali."

"You went in for just two seconds and ran back yelling out like hell, 'The curtains are alive!'" Aarav reminded him.

"I stand by that," Chintu said. "They moved. On their own."

"I think the windows were open," Riya said dryly.

The group laughed as they walked, but they became quiet when they reached the place where the road split—one way went through the haunted tree, and the other was a longer path that felt safer.

They all paused.

"I still think it's just a very ugly tree," Aarav muttered, peering toward the forest.

"You know, from this angle, it looks like it's grinning," Bunty whispered. "Like it knows we're talking about it."

"Great. Now I won't be able to sleep tonight," said Chintu.

Rohan looked at the path thoughtfully. "Imagine if we could just walk through here like normal kids. No ghost, no detour, no late days."

"We'd get an extra hour of sleep," Riya said.

"And I can use that time to build something cool and innovative," Aarav nodded. "Maybe a torch that shoots ghosts through its laser beams.

"I'd write jokes," said Rohan. "Start my own comedy show. Call it. "Haunted kahaniyan."

"I'd just not cry in the mornings," Bunty said honestly.

"You still might," Chintu said with a smile.

"You all laugh now," Bunty said, eyes narrowing. "But when that haunted tree turns one of us into a pigeon, don't say I didn't warn you,"

"You think it turns people into pigeons, really?" Aarav asked.

"It's possible!" Bunty said. "Ghosts are powerful, and they do weird things!"

They were still arguing, and suddenly a gust of wind passed, rustling the leaves of a distant tree. All five froze for a second, then laughed nervously.

"Okay, that was just wind," said Rohan, thumping his chest.

"I knew that," Bunty mumbled, getting a bit closer to Riya.

They started walking again, slower now, but still chatting.

"Seriously, if it is just an old tree… why does no one go near it?" Riya said quietly.

Aarav looked thoughtful. "Maybe someone started the rumour to keep people away. Maybe it's hiding something under or around it."

"Like what?" Chintu asked.

"Treasure? A secret lab! A really lazy guard dog?"

"Or maybe..." Bunty began dramatically, "it's just bored... and wants friends."

The other rolled their eyes.

"Bunty, if that tree wants friends, it should stop scaring away children," said Rohan.

The group burst out laughing again, the tension briefly forgotten.

They still don't know what they would do, but that day, something had changed. A seed of curiosity had been planted in their minds, quietly growing with every step they took away from the shortcut and the tree that watched from afar.

Or maybe... just maybe... The tree was waiting too.

CHAPTER 3

THE IDEA

Summer vacations had arrived in Sambhar, and with them came two things every child craved: freedom and sleep. The mornings were no longer filled with rushed footsteps and half-tied shoelaces. Instead, yawns echoed in the village lanes like musical notes, and dupattas flew in the breeze as mothers tried to drag their kids out of bed.

In one particular lane, the Fantastic Five had shifted so drastically that they declared a "no waking up before 10AM" rule. Their sleep schedules had shifted so drastically that even the village rooster seemed confused, crowing into an empty courtyard.

Aarav, sprawled across his bed with one leg hanging off the side and his pillow covering half his face, suddenly sat up.

"I've figured it out," he whispered to himself, then rubbed his eyes. "I've really figured it out."

Two minutes later, he was on a mission. He dragged himself into his slippers—one green, one blue—brushed only the front two teeth, and dashed out the door.

The others were gathered at their usual summer spot—Rohan's rooftop. With cold lemonade, a noisy fan, and an umbrella made from a broken school project, the roof had transformed into their official headquarters.

Riya was reading a mystery novel. Bunty was trying to make his chips last longer by breaking each into tiny bits. Chintu was solving a puzzle magazine meant for adults. Rohan was practicing a speech he planned to give at the next Independence Day event, whether anyone wanted him to or not.

And then came Aarav—breathless, wild-haired, and grinning like someone who had just discovered gold.

"I know how we can keep sleeping even after school starts," he announced.

"You invented a time machine?" Riya asked without looking up from her book.

"No, something better," Aarav said, flopping down on the mat. "We solve the mystery of the haunted tree."

The group paused. Even the fan slows down for a second.

"Oh no," Bunty groaned, "not this way again."

"Think about it," Aarav said, sitting up straighter. "If we prove the tree isn't haunted, we can use the shortcut. If we use the shortcut, we save more than an hour every day. That's 30 extra minutes of sleep in the morning and 30 more in the evening!"

"That's... math I like," Rohan nodded. "Sleep-based motivation. I respect it."

Chintu tapped his chin. "Also, less walking means less shoe damage. My slippers are on their final warning."

"But... it's still the Haunted Tree," Bunty said, his voice dropping to a whisper. "What if the ghost doesn't like visitors?"

Riya closed her book. "Bunty, the only thing scarier than that tree is missing the school van in front of our teachers. I vote we at least think about it."

Aarav clapped once, proudly. "This is what I'm saying! The tree has been haunting us without even moving. No proof, no ghost, just fear."

"We'd have to investigate," Rohan said, already slipping into manager mode.

"And snacks," Bunty added quickly. "We'll need snacks. Ghost hunting burns calories."

"I'll carry a stick," Chintu said, pulling one from behind his chair. "Just in case."

Riya looked at Aarav. "You really think there's nothing there?"

"I think... something's there," he replied. "But it's not what we think. And I bet it's not supernatural."

"Could be a monkey," Chintu suggested.

"Or an owl," Rohan offered.

"Or a tree that learned to sing from listening to the villagers," Bunty said, instantly earning stares.

"What?" He shrugged. "It could happen."

They all laughed, the rooftop echoing with summer cheer and ridiculous theories. But behind the jokes was a growing sense of excitement.

For years, they had heard stories. Whispers of glowing eyes and eerie music. Warnings passed down like bedtime tales. But never had anyone tried to actually find the truth?

Maybe it was the heat. Maybe it was the boredom. Or maybe it was just that mix of curiosity and courage that only children seem to carry.

That afternoon, the Fantastic Five made a silent decision—one that didn't need a vote or a show of hands. It was written in their eyes and the way they leaned in closer, as Aarav began outlining a rough plan on a piece of paper stained with mango pickle.

They weren't sure what they would find.

Maybe a strange noise. Maybe a hidden nest. Maybe just an ordinary tree covered in an extraordinary number of stories.

But whatever it was, it would be their adventure.

The lemonade glasses were emptied. The fan creaked. The sun dipped slightly, casting longer shadows across the floor.

"So… when do we go?" Chintu finally asked.

Aarav smiled.

"Soon," he said. "But this time, we don't take the long road. We go straight through the heart of the mystery."

And so, the idea was born—not just to slave or solve a rumour—but to do something no one in Sambhar had dared in years.

To walk right up to fear, knock on its bark, and say, "We're not afraid of you anymore."

CHAPTER 4

THE FIRST ATTEMPT

It was a lazy summer afternoon when Rohan dramatically rolled out an old bedsheet in his courtyard and declared, "It's time we go undercover."

Everyone gathered around as if they were about to plan a space mission. Chintu sat with a notepad. Aarav had brought a stick and kept calling it a "pointer." Riya had tied her hair back into a tight ponytail that meant serious business. Bunty arrived five minutes late and dramatically announced, "I have brought salt."

"Why?" Rohan blinked.

"To throw on the ghost," Bunty replied. "Everyone knows ghosts hate salt. I saw it in the *Bhoot* movie."

Riya sighed. "That's not how science—or ghosts—work."

"I'll bring holy water too," Bunty added quickly. "Just in case salt isn't strong enough."

"Can we please start?" Aarav said, tapping his pointer stick on the ground like a teacher.

He drew a crooked circle on the bedsheet using a red crayon.

"This," he said proudly, "is the tree."

"It looks like a potato," Chintu said.

"It's a representation," Aarav huffed.

"Okay, okay," Rohan interrupted. "Mission plan. We go tonight. After dinner. Everyone will be asleep. No one will question where we are. No adults. No suspicious looks."

"Just us," Riya nodded.

"In the dark," Bunty gulped.

"At night," Aarav said with an evil grin.

"With ghosts," Bunty whimpered.

"*Possibly* ghosts," Chintu corrected. "Probably just rats."

"Oh, rats are worse!" Bunty squealed.

"Alright!" Aarav stood up. "We need to list what we are taking. Write it down, Chintu."

Chintu opened his notepad and titled the page: *Mission: Ghost Tree – Essentials*

"One: Torches," Aarav said. "Each of us must carry one."

"Mine's shaped like a dolphin," Rohan added proudly.

"Two: Whistles," Aarav continued. "In case we get separated."

Rohan waved his whistle. "This is always ready. I even cleaned it with toothpaste this morning."

"Three: Snacks," Chintu wrote. "Because ghosts or not, we'll get hungry."

"I vote for aloo chips and mango barfi," Bunty said. "Also, glucose biscuits. They make me brave."

"Four: Notebook," Riya added. "To write down observations. I'll bring my old tuition diary."

"Five: Disguises," Rohan whispered, looking very excited.

Everyone stared.

"Why would we need disguises?" Riya asked.

"In case someone spots us. We'll be the Mystery Mangoes."

"The what?" Chintu said.

"I already made a badge," Rohan said, pulling out a sticker with a very lumpy mango drawn on it.

"Focus!" Aarav snapped. "Number six: Rope."

"Why rope?" Bunty asked.

"In case we fall into a well. Or need to climb. Or… it just feels cool to carry a rope," Aarav said.

"Seven: Salt," Chintu muttered, writing it down for Bunty's satisfaction.

"Eight: Neem leaves, just in case," Riya added.

"Number nine," Bunty said solemnly, "Hanuman Chalisa."

Everyone nodded respectfully.

"And ten," Aarav smiled, "courage."

"I might leave that at home," Bunty whispered.

They spent the next hour stuffing all their "mission gear" into Rohan's old school bag, which now looked like it might explode. Aarav's ghost detector (made from an old TV remote and two blinking fairy lights) was carefully placed on top like a sacred artifact.

At exactly 9:45 PM, the five slipped out of their homes in full stealth mode. Aarav wore all black (including socks on his hands for some reason), Riya had a scarf tied around her face like a detective, Rohan had painted black lines under his eyes like a cricketer, Chintu was wearing his dad's gardening hat, and Bunty… had put his shirt on backwards in panic.

They met near the well behind Rohan's house, their torches off, their hearts racing.

"Everyone ready?" Rohan whispered.

"Wait," Bunty said, "I forgot my water bottle."

"We're not going to some school picnic!" Riya hissed.

"I get nervous thirst," Bunty explained.

Chintu rolled his eyes. "Let's just go before Bunty gets nervous hunger too."

They tiptoed through the village, staying behind walls and bushes, ducking every time a scooter passed. At one point, a goat coughed and Bunty nearly fainted.

Finally, they reached the entrance of the forest path—the same shortcut that led to the haunted tree.

It was darker than they expected. The moon peeked shyly through the clouds, and the trees rustled softly as if whispering secrets. The trail looked exactly the same as in the day… and yet entirely different.

"Flashlights," Aarav commanded.

They all clicked theirs on.

Except Bunty, whose torch made a weak dying noise and went out.

"It's okay," Bunty said, already clinging to Chintu. "I'll hold on to someone."

"You're pulling my shirt," Chintu whispered.

"Sorry. I panic-hug."

They began walking slowly, staying close. Every crunch of leaves underfoot sounded like thunder. Every rustle of branches made Bunty jump. Rohan tried to whistle casually, but ended up sounding like a broken pressure cooker.

"I think I stepped on a bone," Bunty cried.

"It's a stick," Riya said.

"Don't insult the dead," Bunty replied.

Aarav, meanwhile, was scanning the surroundings with his fake ghost detector, which beeped randomly every time it got near Chintu's metal slingshot.

They reached the spot where the tree came into view—and suddenly, everything felt still.

No wind. No sound. Just them… and the tree.

It stood tall, darker than night, its branches stretched wide like arms caught mid-scream. The bark looked rougher. Older. And somehow, angrier.

No one spoke.

Until Rohan whispered, "It looks… bigger at night."

"I think it's breathing," Bunty said.

"It's not breathing," Aarav whispered back. "Trees don't breathe like that."

"I heard it snore," Bunty whispered back.

They all crouched behind a bush, peeking out. Aarav pulled out his notebook. Riya started recording. Chintu had his slingshot ready, though no one knew why. Rohan reached into his bag for the whistle.

And Bunty?

Bunty was mumbling prayers under his breath, clutching his salt pouch like it was pure gold.

They stared at the tree in silence, their hearts loud, their mouths dry.

Nothing moved.

No ghosts appeared.

No voices whispered.

And yet, in the stillness… the tree watched.

It didn't have eyes. But it watched.

Aarav nodded. "Let's go a bit closer. Observe the soil. Look for anything strange—scratches, tools, maybe signs of digging."

The group moved slowly. The silence around them thickened. A cool breeze blew, and a few dry leaves spiralled down.

Suddenly, Bunty's shoe caught on a root.

"AHHHH!"

He flew forward like a missile, waving his arms wildly, and landed head-first into what looked like a muddy ditch hidden behind some fallen leaves.

There was a long silence.

Then a loud wail.

"MY BACK! MY KNEE! I'VE BEEN ATTACKED BY THE EARTH!"

"Bunty's down!" yelled Rohan. "Mission abort!"

"Something touched me! I think it's a ghost!"

"It's a frog," Riya said, peering in with her torch.

"THE FROG IS POSSESSED!" Bunty screamed, now completely coated in mud, thrashing like a hero in a bad soap opera.

Aarav leaned over. "It's just a pit. Probably made by animals. Or rain. Or bad luck."

Chintu tried to help pull Bunty out but slipped and nearly joined him. "I told you we needed a ladder!"

"Why would we carry a ladder into the jungle at night?" Riya shouted.

"Enough!" Rohan screamed, blowing his whistle like an alarm. "Operation Cancelled! I repeat—Operation *Bhootwala Ped* Abort!"

They all grabbed Bunty—muddy, dramatic, and crying like a baby goat—and ran as fast as their slippered feet could go.

They didn't stop until they reached Rohan's courtyard. Panting and sweating, they dropped down on the ground.

Bunty moaned dramatically. "I almost died. I saw a white light. It was Riya's torch, but still..."

"You didn't die," Aarav said. "You just found a hidden ditch with your whole face."

Riya handed him a towel. "Congratulations. You've officially become the first human mud ball."

"You guys left me behind!" Bunty accused.

"You were screaming too much. We could still hear you while running," Chintu said.

"That's called teamwork," Rohan added. "You scream; we run."

"I hate this mission," Bunty muttered.

"I kinda loved it," Riya said. "We didn't get to the tree, but that fall was legendary."

The Fantastic Five sat in silence for a moment, still buzzing with adrenaline.

They had failed. They hadn't cracked the mystery. But somehow... it felt like the beginning of something bigger.

And somewhere far off, deep in the forest, the tree stood tall and silent—as if smirking.

CHAPTER 5

THE CLUE NOBODY SAW

After Bunty's Great Mud Incident, the Fantastic Five took a silent oath not to go anywhere near the haunted tree for a while. For the next week, they didn't even pass by the forest road during the day. Bunty, for one, refused to eat anything that even looked like mud.

"I'm still traumatized," he'd declare dramatically, pointing to his elbow. "This bruise glows in the dark—I swear."

"That's a mosquito bite," Chintu would mutter.

But beneath all the jokes and drama, something had indeed changed. The tree had challenged them. And nobody liked losing—especially not Rohan, who had started referring to the failed mission as *"The Tragedy of the Ghost Ditch."*

They needed a better plan. A smarter plan. A non-muddy plan.

The idea began, as all great village ideas do, near the old Paani Tanki, where they sat one lazy afternoon, each clutching a glass of orange Rasana.

"We went in blind," Aarav said, sketching something with a stick in the sand. "No real prep. No backup. And no logic."

"We had salt," Bunty reminded him, as if that had been their biggest weapon.

"Exactly. That was the problem," Riya said, squinting up at the sun.

"We need to observe from a distance first," Chintu added, "like spies—not like panicked chickens running through mud."

"I wasn't panicking," Bunty said. "I was expressing high-pitched concern."

"You were screeching like a banshee," Rohan smirked.

But the planning had started. Aarav pulled out his mission notebook again. It still had mango pickle stains, but now the heading read: *"Operation Ghost Tree 2.0."*

"Here's what we do," Aarav began. "We don't go straight to the tree. We study it from a distance over a few days. Observe everything—sounds, lights, smells."

"Smells?" Rohan raised an eyebrow.

"Ghosts might smell like burnt pakoras. You never know," Aarav replied solemnly.

"We can take turns sitting on Babloo uncle's abandoned tractor near the forest edge," Chintu said. "It's the perfect spot."

"Oh yes!" Riya clapped. "That tractor's been there since the last monsoon. Nobody even looks at it anymore. It's practically invisible."

"We'll bring binoculars," Rohan nodded. "Well, toy binoculars. Mine are made of two empty Fevicol bottles, but they kind of work."

"Do we need disguises again?" Bunty asked, already sweating.

"No," Riya rolled her eyes. "You wore your shirt backward last time. That was not a disguise. That was laundry failure."

"Fine. But this time, we bring better snacks. I vote samosas," Bunty said. "Samosas give me focus."

"Samosas give you gas," Chintu corrected.

"And gas gives me energy," Bunty countered proudly.

They laughed, agreed to meet that evening, and one by one, scattered back to their homes.

That night, Rohan brought a blanket and two stools to Babloo uncle's old tractor. Aarav came with a pencil torch and a pair of walkie-talkies made from empty matchboxes (that worked about as well as whispering into a tree). Riya brought a notepad, while Chintu brought a compass that only pointed west no matter where you turned it. Bunty? He brought samosas. And two boiled eggs. For "extra protein," he claimed.

Their first night was uneventful—unless you count Rohan accidentally sitting on a lizard, which led to a scream so loud that someone in the next village asked if a peacock was laying an egg.

But the second night brought something strange.

While Aarav was pretending to be asleep to test everyone's alertness, Riya pointed toward the tree and whispered, "Look! Did you see that?"

A faint shimmer. A flicker. Like someone had waved a mirror.

Everyone froze. Even Bunty paused mid-samosa.

"Was that… light?" Chintu whispered.

"No moonlight can reflect like that," Aarav said, alert now.

"It came from the left side of the tree," Rohan noted, squinting. "Near the roots."

"There it is again!" Riya whispered.

They all leaned forward—five heads stacked like a human tower of paranoia.

And then… nothing.

It stopped. The tree stood still, quiet, like it had always been.

But something was different.

The next evening, they returned. This time, they brought magnifying glasses (actually Chintu's mother's old reading glasses) and one of Rohan's mom's steel thalis to reflect light in Morse code—just in case the ghost wanted to chat.

Again, around the same time, the flicker came.

Not just once. Twice.

"Same spot!" Aarav said, excitedly scribbling in the notebook.

They kept watching. On the fourth night, Aarav brought a plastic mirror to reflect light at the tree.

To everyone's shock, the tree flickered back.

"What WAS THAT?" Bunty shrieked. "It responded! We've made contact! We are doomed!"

"No, wait..." Riya stood up. "That's not magic—it's reflection. Something shiny is there."

They all exchanged looks.

Aarav's voice trembled with excitement. "We're not imagining it. Something shiny is reflecting light near the base of the tree. It's not ghostly—it's metallic."

"Buried treasure?" Chintu said, eyes wide.

"Tools?" Rohan offered.

"Gold biscuits?" Bunty whispered.

"Stop thinking about food," Riya muttered.

"Not food! Actual gold biscuits," Bunty corrected, licking his fingers anyway.

The Fantastic Five sat quietly. Their earlier fear had now melted into something else—curiosity. Big, undeniable, delicious curiosity.

The haunted tree wasn't just creepy. It was hiding something.

And someone had tried to hide it well.

That night, Aarav wrote a lot in his notebook:

"There's something buried or hidden near the haunted tree. Possibly something shiny. Someone comes there and checks it sometimes—maybe every few nights. That's what we've been seeing. Not a ghost. A person."

They had found their first real clue.

But now came the bigger decision—what to do next.

"We go," Rohan said. "Tomorrow night."

"We go prepared," Riya added. "Gloves. Torches. Something to dig. Rope."

"And samosas," Bunty said automatically.

"No samosas," Chintu groaned.

"Okay… kachoris," Bunty bargained.

"Fine, but only one each. We're clue detectives now, not picnic planners," Riya sighed.

"Speak for yourself. I plan to do both," Bunty grinned.

The five sat under the stars, eyes sparkling, stomachs rumbling, and hearts pounding with excitement. Their failed first mission had turned into something bigger. They were no longer ghost hunters—they were clue detectives now.

And this time… they wouldn't fall into a muddy pit.

Probably.

CHAPTER 6

THE SECRET BENEATH THE ROOTS

It was the fifth night of their mission.

The Fantastic Five were now self-declared experts in jungle surveillance. That evening, the group assembled with unmatched seriousness.

Rohan carried a gardener's spade he had borrowed without really asking. Aarav brought a plastic tiffin box filled with "tools" – mostly spoons, a broken screwdriver, and one butter knife. Riya wore gloves like a forensic scientist. Chintu had made an "evidence bag" out of a washed milk packet. And Bunty? Bunty came armed with mosquito repellent, four bananas, and a packet of cream rolls "for emergency ghost encounters." He also wore two pairs of socks, claiming they were ghost-proof.

They crept through the fields like clumsy, oversized squirrels. Every few steps, Bunty tripped over his own socks and whispered, "Sorry, sorry," as if apologizing to invisible spirits.

They finally reached the haunted tree's territory.

It looked just as it always had – angry, ancient, and utterly unfriendly. Its bark was darker than burnt roti, and its twisted branches resembled claws ready to snatch careless adventurers.

"Everyone ready?" Rohan whispered.

"No," Bunty replied immediately.

"Perfect," Riya said, marching forward anyway.

They approached the same spot near the base of the tree where they had seen the mysterious shimmer the previous nights. The soil looked uneven.

Aarav knelt. "It's loose… someone's been digging here."

"Maybe a ghost with a shovel?" Bunty offered.

"Or just a regular human with two working arms," Riya replied.

Without wasting time, they began digging. Rohan dug like he was competing in a village Olympics. Aarav used two spoons with surgical precision. Riya worked swiftly, and Chintu kept moving the flashlights so much it felt like they were in a disco. Bunty, meanwhile, was patting nearby soil randomly, whispering, "Maybe the treasure moved."

CLINK!

Chintu's spoon struck something hard.

"Bone?" Bunty whispered.

"Nope. Metal," Riya said excitedly.

They cleared the soil away, revealing the edge of a small, rusty metal box. It was dusty, dented, and definitely very old.

Rohan carefully opened it using Aarav's broken screwdriver. The lid creaked like it hadn't seen daylight since dinosaurs went extinct.

Inside… were coins. Dusty, round, some golden, some not, and all strange-looking. And under those coins… a folded yellow paper.

"A note!" Riya gasped. "This could be a key to everything!"

She carefully unfolded the paper… and then squinted.

"Wait… this isn't Hindi," she muttered. "What language is this?"

Everyone leaned in.

The paper was covered in curly letters and strange curves.

"Is this Urdu?" Rohan asked.

"No, no, it's not that," Aarav said, rubbing his chin. "It's not Punjabi either."

"It's definitely not English," Bunty said, proudly contributing nothing.

"I think… I think it's Sanskrit," Chintu announced.

"Sanskrit?!" Bunty looked horrified. "You mean the ancient stuff they used in temple bhajans or old movie chants?"

"Yes," Riya said, frowning. "Which means…"

"No one here can read it," Aarav sighed.

Everyone stared at the mysterious note like it was a math exam.

"This is cruel," Rohan said. "Someone leaves us a legendary treasure and writes the instructions in a language we only see on school walls."

"Maybe it says, this treasure will explode in 60 seconds," Bunty whimpered

"Don't be dramatic," Riya said. "It probably just says whose it is."

"Or… how cursed it is," Bunty whispered again.

They looked around, unsure what to do.

"We can't take it to the police," Chintu said. "They'll ask questions."

"We can't leave it here either," Rohan added. "What if someone else finds it?"

"We could bury it again and guard it in shifts," Aarav suggested.

"I can't stay up all night guarding gold. I have a delicate sleep cycle," Bunty said. "Also… what if it calls to other ghosts?"

"Ghosts don't use Google Translate, Bunty," Riya snapped.

Finally, after many intense discussions and two more cream rolls, they decided to temporarily hide the box at Rohan's house. His Dadi had the deepest cupboard in the village – once, she lost a pressure cooker in it for two months.

Rohan wrapped the box in a towel, stuffed it in a steel dabba, and then tucked that inside an old school bag labelled: "CLASS 3 Homework – DO NOT TOUCH."

"No ghost will dare open this," he said proudly.

"True," said Bunty. "Even I wouldn't touch old homework."

Back at Rohan's house, they tiptoed into his room like professional burglars. Dadi was watching her TV serial, yelling at the villain on screen, so no one noticed the five children sneaking in with treasure like it was pickles from someone else's tiffin.

The box was hidden under a pile of science books and a broken globe. They all sat down, panting, sweaty, and overwhelmed.

"I can't believe this," Aarav said. "The haunted tree… it was guarding a treasure."

"Or hiding a secret," Riya corrected.

"And someone tried to keep people away by telling ghost stories," Chintu added. "It worked for years."

"I KNEW IT!" Bunty shouted. "I said it didn't feel like a real ghost zone. It was too dusty. Ghosts like clean places."

Everyone ignored him.

"So, what now?" Riya asked. "Do we try to decode the Sanskrit?"

"We could go to Pandit ji," Aarav said. "He reads Sanskrit."

"Absolutely not," Rohan said. "He'll tell our parents. Then we'll be haunted by chappals."

"Dadaji at the library maybe?" Chintu suggested. "He knows weird things."

"Yes!" Riya agreed. "He reads those ancient books no one touches. He might help."

"We'll go tomorrow," Rohan declared. "Daylight. With snacks."

"No samosas this time," Chintu said sternly.

"I vote for kachoris," Bunty said.

"Fine, but one each," Riya warned. "We're solving mysteries, not organizing a wedding buffet."

They laughed and high-fived each other, still buzzing with excitement.

Outside, the tree stood silently, its dark branches swaying gently in the night breeze. It no longer felt terrifying—just old. Mysterious. And oddly relieved, as if happy that its secret had finally been discovered.

Inside Rohan's cupboard, the gold box waited quietly.

Tomorrow, they'd take the next step.

But tonight, the Fantastic Five had done something magical – not just cracked a legend, but turned fear into friendship, mystery into mission, and the haunted tree into just another story waiting to be told.

And somewhere deep in his heart, even Bunty admitted…

This was better than cream rolls.

Probably.

CHAPTER 7

THE GOLD THAT SPOKE IN PUZZLES

The next morning, all five of them woke up earlier than ever – even Bunty didn't hit snooze on an alarm (mainly because he never set one). The excitement of the mysterious Sanskrit letter was just too strong. Who had written it? What did it say? Could it be a warning? A secret map? Or a very old menu?

They gathered at Riya's veranda and marched directly to the library – one carrying the letter, one with a backpack full of bananas, one holding a notebook of clues, one wearing gloves (again), and Bunty... well, Bunty had brought a tiny bottle of sanitizer "just in case ghosts had germs."

The village library was quiet as always, the kind of quiet where even a sneeze felt illegal. Dadaji sat at his desk, wrapped in a shawl despite the heat, sipping what could only be his hundredth cup of tea for the day. A stack of books towered beside him like a leaning tower of wisdom.

"Namaste, Dadaji," Aarav said politely.

"Ah, the detectives return," Dadaji smiled. "What mystery have you solved today?"

Rohan stepped forward. "We found this letter, Dadaji, at my home in a cupboard, but the problem is… it's in Sanskrit. We were hoping you could help us read it."

At the mention of Sanskrit, Dadaji's eyebrow danced. He adjusted his glasses, pulled out a magnifying glass, and flipped open a dusty book titled *Sanskrit for Nerds and Legends.* He began muttering to himself as he scanned the letter.

The kids waited. Riya bit her nails. Aarav bounced on his toes. Chintu stared at a bookshelf so long he swore one of the books blinked. Bunty discovered a cobweb that looked like a spider had written "Go away" in code.

Finally, Dadaji looked up, his eyes twinkling.

"This is not just a letter," he said. "It's a message. A very old one. Possibly written during the time of great political unrest… or a family dispute."

Everyone leaned in as Dadaji cleared his throat and read aloud in a soft, serious voice:

"This gold is not stolen
It is the legacy of my family.
I bury it here, not to hide it, but to protect it.
The world is not ready.
When it is found by kind hands, let it serve a purpose.
If you are reading this,
Do not waste this gold.
Do not fight over it.
Use it wisely."

The room fell silent. Even Bunty didn't speak – which itself was a historic event.

"I thought it would be something scary," Aarav said softly.

"Or a warning about angry spirits," Riya added.

Bunty finally spoke. "So… it's emotional gold? Not cursed gold? That's way less dramatic."

Chintu tilted his head. "He buried it to protect it from the British, or from people who were trying to steal it."

Rohan looked thoughtful. "It's not just treasure. It's trust."

They left the library in a daze, without explaining anything to Dadaji. What started as a ghost hunt was now a gold quest… with morals. The letter had changed everything. It wasn't about shiny coins anymore. It was about responsibility.

"So… what do we do now?" Chintu asked as they gathered in Rohan's room.

"We can't keep it," Riya said. "It's not ours."

"But it is ours," Bunty argued, his face scrunched in confusion. "I mean… we found it. That counts for something, right?"

"Bunty, this isn't a lucky coin you find on the road. This is centuries-old gold with a heart-touching poem!" Aarav said, waving the letter in the air dramatically.

Chintu flopped onto Rohan's bed, arms wide like he had just carried the gold himself across three deserts. "Should we bury it again? Maybe it's safest that way. Like a time capsule for the next generation of confused children."

"No way!" Rohan protested. "What if someone else finds it and uses it to build a giant statue of themselves or… or opens a shop that only sells socks?"

Bunty gasped. "A sock shop with no customers! The horror!"

"Focus!" Riya clapped her hands. "We have three options. One, we give it to our parents. Two, we give it to the Sarpanch ji. Three, we keep it hidden and pretend this morning never happened."

They all stared at her like she'd just turned into a talking pineapple.

"I vote parents," Aarav said finally. "They're responsible. Except my dad, who once ate an entire chilli thinking it was a tomato."

"Sarpanch ji is more official," Rohan said. "He might know what to do with something this valuable."

"What if we call the news?" Bunty offered. "We'll be famous! The Fantastic Five! On TV! With subtitles!"

"Bunty," Riya groaned. "This isn't about selfies and spotlights!"

There was silence again. Rohan paced the room; the letter now folded neatly in his palm like it was the most delicate thing in the world.

"I feel like we're sitting on a moral volcano," he muttered.

"Maybe we should ask Dadaji what he thinks?" Aarav suggested. "He knows about history, about legacies… about not panicking when holding ancient secrets."

"But then he'll definitely tell our parents," Riya said. "He's from the 'no secrets after snacks' generation."

"Let's take a vote," Chintu said, sitting up.

- **Rohan**: Sarpanch ji.
- **Riya**: Parents.
- **Aarav**: Dadaji.
- **Chintu**: Bury it.
- **Bunty**: News channel with dramatic music.

They stared at one another.

"Well," Riya sighed, "we're officially confused."
"We need a plan," Rohan said.
"We need snacks," Bunty corrected.
"Both," Aarav added. "And a nap. My brain feels like mashed potatoes."

Chintu slowly rolled off the bed, looking like an exhausted old man who'd lived too many lives in one morning. "Let's sleep on it. No one's chasing us for the gold. Yet."

They agreed, reluctantly. The gold stayed hidden – tucked safely under a loose wooden plank in Rohan's room for the night – guarded only by a sock and Bunty's sanitizer bottle.

The Fantastic Five had uncovered a treasure, unlocked a mystery, and read a forgotten letter from a forgotten time… but now they were stuck in the biggest mystery of all:

They had solved the puzzle, but the biggest question remained – what to do with the answer?

CHAPTER 8

THE GOLD THAT CHANGED EVERYTHING

The Fantastic Five were gathered in Riya's veranda again – the same place where this whole madness had begun. But this time, they weren't whispering ghost stories or passing around magnifying glasses. They were holding a shiny box full of gold coins and a handwritten note that still smelled like mystery and mild panic.

"So… we agree?" asked Rohan, looking at the others like a class monitor confirming homework submissions.

"Yes," Riya nodded. "We need to tell Sarpanch Ji. It's time the village knew the truth."

"I still think we should open a pizza place with the gold," Bunty mumbled, biting into a dry roti. "But okay… honesty is the best policy."

"Good," Aarav said. "Let's go now. Before Bunty eats one of the coins thinking it's a golden biscuit."

Chintu was already packing the box gently in his school bag, cushioning it with a towel that smelled vaguely of his grandmother's hair oil.

So off they went – marching like a team of heroes who had just come out of a jungle expedition. Which, to be fair, they had.

Sarpanch Ji was lounging on his charpai outside his house, sipping chai and solving the day's most difficult Sudoku puzzle (he was still on box three). When he saw the kids arrive, all looking suspiciously serious and clean for a bunch of supposed ghost-hunters, he raised an eyebrow.

"What's this? A science project?" he joked.

"No, Sarpanch Ji," Riya began, with the confidence of a lawyer in a courtroom. "It's a truth project."

And so, they narrated the entire tale – from the ghost rumours, late-night spying missions, and jungle digging, to the letter hidden with the gold.

By the time they finished, Sarpanch Ji's chai had gone cold and his mouth had gone dry.

"You're telling me… all this time… the ghost was just a rumour to hide gold?"

"Yes!" said Chintu. "And it worked really well. I didn't sleep properly for three weeks!"

"Hmm…" Sarpanch Ji stood up slowly and looked at them, nodding thoughtfully. "Bacchon, you've shown courage, cleverness… and a mild disregard for jungle safety laws. But I'm proud. You've done what most adults wouldn't have dared to."

Bunty beamed. "Does that mean we get a reward?"

"You'll get laddoos," the Sarpanch promised, "and maybe a statue."

"YESSS!" Bunty fist-pumped the air.

The very next day, a grand Panchayat was called in the village. People gathered under the giant neem tree, confused about what could be so important. Ramu Chacha had even brought his buffalo along, thinking it was a free food distribution.

Sarpanch Ji stood up and cleared his throat like a politician about to declare a national holiday.

"People of our village," he began dramatically. "There is no ghost."

Gasps. Loud enough to scare an actual ghost, had there been one.

"Yes, you heard me right. The haunted tree .. was never haunted. Instead, it was hiding a treasure – a box of gold buried by a noble soul many years ago. It was protected by fear… until these brave children uncovered the truth."

He pointed proudly at the Fantastic Five, who were now standing on a raised platform. Bunty waved like a film star, while Chintu nervously checked his shoelaces.

"They did not steal it. They did not hide it. They came straight to me. That… is bravery with brains," the Sarpanch declared.

The villagers broke into loud applause.

After much clapping and some celebratory samosas, it was decided that the gold would be handed over to the police. But not just quietly – oh no. The handover was done with full camera coverage, news reporters, and one local man who kept walking into the camera shot trying to wave at his relatives on TV.

The authorities confirmed that the gold wasn't stolen. The note with the gold – "Use it for those who cannot fight for themselves" – melted everyone's hearts. Especially Inspector Verma, who cried a little but blamed it on dust.

Soon after, the government announced the creation of a museum – right near the tree, in honour of the buried treasure and the Fantastic Five. It was called the *Tree of Truth Museum.* Fancy, right?

The museum displayed the gold, the note (now laminated and framed), the kids' drawings, and even Bunty's muddy sock from the jungle night (somehow declared 'historic evidence'). Tourists poured in from nearby cities, clicking selfies with the tree, the kids' statues, and a suspicious-looking squirrel.

And guess what? Every ticket sold brought money into the village. And that money? Not wasted.

New classrooms were built in the school. The water pump was fixed. Streetlights glowed at night. A new clinic was opened – with Chintu's name on the thermometer box because he once fainted just from digging.

Rohan's dream of an annual "Adventure Day" at school came true. Riya got a reading corner filled with books on real-life detectives. Aarav helped the school start a science club. Chintu proudly became head of the "Safety Squad," making sure no one brought laddoos into the lab. And Bunty… well, Bunty started a fan club called "Banana Avengers." Don't ask why.

One evening, as they sat once again near the not-so-haunted tree, Bunty said, "I still wish there was a ghost. That would've made the museum cooler."

"But then we wouldn't be heroes," Riya teased.

"We'd be… ghost snacks," added Aarav.

"Or ghost poop," said Chintu. Everyone laughed.

Rohan grinned. "From ghost busting to gold trusting – what a journey!"

They all leaned back, watching the lights of the museum twinkle through the leaves. The village was no longer scared of the tree. In fact, people now hugged it and took selfies.

The Fantastic Five had done something extraordinary – not just found treasure, but turned fear into pride, and a ghost story into a golden future.

And they would never forget it.

EPILOGUE

The Tree That Told the Truth

The old tree now stands taller than ever – not because it grew, but because it's finally proud. No longer feared, it's become the selfie-spot of the village, decorated with fairy lights and a small board that reads: *"No Ghosts. Just History."*

The Fantastic Five went back to being regular kids (well, sort of). They still climbed trees, argued over who ate the last biscuit, and occasionally stared suspiciously at oddly shaped bushes.

But the best part of their heroic adventure? They discovered that the path near the once-'haunted' tree was actually a shortcut to school. No more long walks around the fields. No more waking up before the roosters even opened their eyes. Now, they could sleep in for an extra fifteen minutes every morning – which Bunty proudly called *"The Real Treasure of the Mystery."*

Of course, Bunty still managed to be late sometimes, claiming, *"The tree whispered good morning, so I had to reply. Manners first, school second."*

Whenever someone new visited the museum and asked, *"Wait, kids solved all this?"* the villagers would proudly say, *"Yes. And they didn't even Google it."*

Because some stories don't need magic wands or flying carpets – just a bunch of curious kids, a scary tree, and apparently, the fastest school route in village history.

The End.
(Or maybe… the beginning of their next big mystery?)

NO GHOSTS.
JUST HISTORY.